Copyright © 1981, Verlag Neugebauer Press, Salzburg, Austria.
Original title: Das fremde Kind
Copyright © 1984, English text, Neugebauer Press USA Inc.
Published in USA by Neugebauer Press USA Inc.,
Distributed by Alphabet Press, Natick, MA.
Distributed in Canada by Vanwell Publishing, St. Catharines, Ontario.
Published in UK by Neugebauer Press Publishing, Ltd., London,
Distributed by A & C Black, London.
Distributed in Australia by Hutchinson Group Australia Pty. Ltd.
All rights reserved.
Printed in Austria

Library of Congress Cataloging in Publication Data
Bell, Anthea.
The strange child.
(Picture book studio USA)
Adaptation of: Das fremde Kind.
Summary: A magical being comes into the unhappy lives
of a brother and sister, leading them into a world of
fantasy and adventure.
1. Children's stories, French. (1. Fairy tales)
I. Zwerger, Lisbeth, ill.   II. Hoffmann, E. T. A. (Ernst
Theodor Amadeus), 1776–1822. Fremde Kind.   III. Title.
IV. Series: Picture book studio.
PZ8.B399St 1984   [E]   84-8404
ISBN 0-907234-60-7

Ask your bookseller for these other Picture Book Studio books
illustrated by Lisbeth Zwerger:

THE NUTCRACKER by E. T. A. Hoffmann
THE GIFT OF THE MAGI by O. Henry
HANSEL & GRETEL by The Brothers Grimm
LITTLE RED CAP by The Brothers Grimm
THE NIGHTINGALE by Hans Christian Andersen
THE SELFISH GIANT by Oscar Wilde
THE SEVEN RAVENS by The Brothers Grimm
THE SWINEHERD by Hans Christian Andersen
THUMBELINE by Hans Christian Andersen

E.T.A. Hoffmann

THE STRANGE CHILD

Illustrated by Lisbeth Zwerger
Translated and adapted by Anthea Bell

PICTURE BOOK STUDIO USA

Once upon a time there was a country gentleman called Sir Thaddeus of Brakel. He had inherited the little village of Brakelheim from his father, and he lived there quietly, much loved by one and all, in a small but comfortable house, with his wife, his son Felix and his daughter Christlieb.

THE GRAND
VISITORS

One morning the whole family rose early. Sir Thaddeus's wife baked a cake full of almonds and raisins, Sir Thaddeus himself put on his good green coat, and Felix and Christlieb had to wear their best clothes too, for there were grand visitors coming: Count Cyprian of Brakel, Sir Thaddeus's cousin, along with his wife and children.

It was a beautiful day, and Felix and Christlieb were sorry they could not run out into the woods to play. Instead, they had to stay indoors waiting for the visitors to arrive.

WHEN THE
GRAND
VISITORS CAME

At last they drove up in a very fine carriage. The Count and his family had elegant manners and were rigged out in the most expensive clothes: young Hermann wore a pair of long trousers and a cap with a feather in it, and had a shiny little sword by his side, and his sister Adelgunde's dress was all covered with ribbons and lace.

Sad to say, the four young cousins did not get along well together. The Count's children were pert and spoiled. They knew all sorts of things about history and geography and zoology, and even astronomy, and they liked to show off their knowledge, while Felix and Christlieb, who had grown up running wild in the forest, felt clumsy and tongue-tied beside them. The Countess exclaimed in amazement at their countrified ignorance, and the Count promised Sir Thaddeus and his lady to send them a tutor to give their children some schooling, saying it would cost them nothing.

Then the coachman carried two big boxes into the house. Adelgunde and Hermann presented them to Christlieb and Felix. "Here are some toys for you, my dear fellow!" said Hermann to his cousin, making him a bow.

Felix felt awkward, and didn't know what to say, and his sister too was closer to tears than smiles, even though the box Adelgunde was giving her smelled delicious, as if it were full of good things to eat. Then Sultan, Felix's faithful dog, began barking and jumping up, and Hermann was so scared that he ran to the far end of the room and started to howl.

"He won't hurt you!" Felix told his cousin. "There's no need to bawl like that –

he's only a dog, and anyway, even if he did attack you, you've got a sword, haven't you?"

But Hermann just kept on howling until the coachman picked him up and carried him out to the carriage. Adelgunde began crying too, for no particular reason, and then so did poor Christlieb, and it was to the sound of three children weeping and wailing that the grand visitors drove away.

THE NEW TOYS Just as soon as the carriage had gone, Sir Thaddeus tore off his good green coat, put on his everyday jacket, ran a big comb through his hair, took a deep breath and stretched. "Well, thank God for that!" said he.

The children took their best clothes off too, feeling happy and carefree. "Come on, let's go out into the forest!" cried Felix.

"Don't you want to look at your presents?" asked their mother. Christlieb had been glancing curiously at the boxes, and she thought that was a good idea, but Felix was not so sure.

"Huh!" he said. "How could Cousin Baggy Breeches have brought us anything nice? He can talk and talk, all about lions and bears and elephants and how much he knows, and then he's scared of Sultan! Howling and bawling and hiding under the table, even though he wears a sword!"

"Oh, Felix dear, do let's just peep inside the boxes!" said Christlieb.

Felix would do anything to please her, so he agreed. His mother opened the boxes and then – well, dear readers, I expect you have all been lucky enough to get lots of lovely presents from your families and friends, at Christmas or on feast days! Remember how you shouted for joy at the sight of those shiny toy soldiers, funny little mechanical men with barrel organs, prettily dressed dolls and colored picture books? That was the way Felix and Christlieb felt, for those boxes were crammed with wonderful toys and delicious things to eat.

"Oh, how lovely!" cried the children, clapping their hands.

The toy Felix liked best was a handsome huntsman who could bring up his rifle and aim it at a target when you pulled a thread at the back of his jacket. Next best was a little man who could make a bow and play a tinkling tune on the harp if you wound him up. And there was a gun, and a hunting knife, both of them made of wood and painted silver, as well as a fine hussar's cap and a cartridge pouch. As for Christlieb, she was delighted with her pretty doll, and a full set of pots and pans. Both children forgot all about going out into the forest, and played with their new toys until it was time for bed.

Next day they took the toys out of their boxes to play with them again. But the
sun was shining in through the window, the birds were singing, and suddenly
Felix cried, "Oh, come along, Christlieb, it's more fun outside after all! We
can take the nicest toys out with us!"

However, the toys seemed less interesting when they were out among the
beauties of Nature, and the children became impatient and played roughly with
them, so that several of them broke, including the huntsman and the harpist.
"Let's have a good run!" said Felix.

"Oh yes!" said Christlieb. "And my pretty doll can run with us."

So they each took the doll by one arm, and off they ran, through the bushes,
down the hill, and on and on until they came to a pond. It was surrounded by
tall reeds, and Sir Thaddeus sometimes shot wild duck there.

"Why don't we stop here for a while?" said Felix. "Maybe I can shoot a duck, just
like Father. After all, I have a gun."

But then Christlieb cried, "Oh, my doll! What's happened to my doll?"

Sure enough, the poor doll was in a bad way! The children had forgotten to be
careful of her as they ran, so her clothes had all been torn by the bushes and both
her legs were broken. Her once pretty wax face was scratched to bits.

"My doll!" wailed Christlieb. "My lovely doll!"

"Well, now you see what silly things our cousins brought us!" said Felix. "Your
doll's no use if she can't even come for a run with us – here, hand her over!"

Sadly, Christlieb gave her brother the damaged doll, but she couldn't help crying
out, "Oh no!" when he simply tossed it into the pond.

"Cheer up!" Felix consoled her. "Don't cry over that stupid doll! If I shoot a
duck I'll give you the prettiest feathers from its wings!"

There was a rustle among the reeds, and Felix raised his wooden gun at once.
Next moment, however, he lowered it again. "I'm a fool!" he said. "You need
powder and shot to fire a gun. I don't have any powder and shot, and even if I
did, how could I load a wooden gun? The hunting knife's no use either. It
doesn't cut! I tell you what – Cousin Baggy Breeches was just making fun of me!
His toys may look very fine, but they're no real good at all."

And so saying, Felix threw his gun, his knife and his cartridge pouch into the
pond.

Poor Christlieb was still grieving for her doll, and Felix was in a bad temper too
as they made their way home. When their mother asked, "Why, children, where
are your toys?" Felix told her straight out how he and Christlieb had been

cheated over the huntsman and the harper, the gun and the knife and the doll.

"Dear me!" said their mother, a little crossly. "You don't know how to play with such pretty, delicate things properly, that's all, you silly children!"

However, Sir Thaddeus said, "Let the children be! I'm glad enough to see them rid of such outlandish toys, which did nothing but bewilder them."

And neither his lady nor the children knew what Sir Thaddeus meant by that!

THE STRANGE CHILD The next day, Felix and Christlieb went out into the forest early. Their mother had told them to be back in good time, because they must do some reading and writing, so as not to disgrace themselves utterly when the new tutor arrived.

"Let's enjoy ourselves while we can!" said Felix. So they began to play a game of "Catch". Yet after a few moments it seemed boring, and so did everything else they played. Nothing would go right. Felix's cap was blown off, and he tripped and fell flat on his face; Christlieb caught her dress on some thorns and stubbed her toe painfully. "I suppose we'd better go home," said Felix crossly, but instead, he threw himself down in the shade of a fine tree, and so did his sister. There they both sat, staring moodily at the ground.

"Oh dear," sighed Christlieb, "if only we still had those lovely toys!"

"They wouldn't do us any good," muttered Felix. "We'd only break them again! Mother was very likely right, Christlieb. There was nothing wrong with those toys, but we're so ignorant we didn't know how to play with them!"

"Yes," agreed Christlieb. "If we are as clever as our cousins, then you'd still have your huntsman and your little harpist, and my lovely doll wouldn't be at the bottom of the pond! Oh, why are we so clumsy and so ignorant!"

She began to sob and weep pitifully, and Felix joined in. They both wept out loud, wailing, "If only we weren't so ignorant!"

Then, all of a sudden, they stopped crying and looked at each other in amazement.

"Do you see that, Christlieb?" asked Felix.

"Do you hear that, Felix?" asked Christlieb.

A wonderful light was glowing among the deep shadows of the dark bush opposite the children. It shone out through the trembling leaves like soft moonbeams, and amidst the rustle of the trees the children heard a sweet sound, like the wind brushing over harpstrings and awakening their slumbering chords with its caress. The children felt very strange. Their grief was all gone and although tears still stood in their eyes, they were tears of a sweet sadness they had

never known before. And as the glowing light grew brighter and the wonderful music sounded louder, the children's hearts beat faster. They stared into the light, and then they saw it was the beautiful face of a lovely child, brightly lit up by the sun, smiling and beckoning to them out of the bush.

"Come here – oh, come here, you dear child!" cried Christlieb and Felix, jumping up and holding out their hands.

"Here I come! Here I come!" cried the child's sweet voice out of the bush, and floating lightly, as if carried upon the morning breeze, it came over to Felix and Christlieb. "I heard you weeping, far away," said the child, "and I felt so sorry for you! Dear children, what is the matter?"

"We weren't quite sure ourselves," said Felix, "but now I think it was just because we missed you!"

"Yes," said Christlieb, "and now you're here we are happy again! Oh, why were you away so long?" For both children really felt as if they had known the strange child forever, and that they had all played together before, and that it was only the loss of their playmate that had made them sad.

"I'm afraid we have no toys," said Felix, "because I was so silly that I spoiled all the nice things my cousin gave me and threw them away; but we can still play games together, can't we?"

"Oh, Felix!" said the strange child, laughing. "The toys you threw away weren't worth much, but you have the most wonderful playthings ever seen here around you!"

"Where? Where are they?" cried Christlieb and Felix.

"Just look about you," said the strange child. Then Felix and Christlieb saw all kinds of beautiful flowers peering bright-eyed out of the thick grass. There were colored pebbles and crystal shells sparkling among them, and little golden beetles, humming softly, danced up and down.

"Let's build a palace! Help me collect some pebbles!" said the strange child, bending to gather up the colored stones. Christlieb and Felix helped, and the strange child built so deftly that tall columns soon rose, shining in the sun like polished metal, with a golden roof arching above them.

The strange child kissed the flowers peering out of the grass, and they rose up with a sweet whispering sound and twined lovingly together to make fragrant arcades, down which the children danced joyfully. Then the child clapped its hands, and the golden palace roof flew apart, humming (for the little golden beetles had made it with their wing cases), the pillars dissolved into a babbling silvery brook, and the flowers lay down upon its banks.

Next, the strange child picked blades of grass and broke some small twigs off the trees. The blades of grass turned into the most beautiful dolls, and the twigs became fine little huntsmen. The dolls danced around Christlieb and then let her take them on her lap, whispering in their tiny voices, "Be kind to us, dear Christlieb!" As for the huntsmen, they bustled about, blowing their horns and rattling their guns, and shouting, "Tally ho! View halloo!" Then little hares jumped out of the bushes, and little hounds went chasing after them, and the huntsmen followed, firing off their guns. What fun it was!

And then everything disappeared. "Oh!" cried Felix and Christlieb. "Where are the dolls? Where are the huntsmen?"

"At your service whenever you want them!" said the strange child. "But wouldn't you like to go walking in the forest now?"

"Yes, yes!" said Felix and Christlieb, so the strange child took their hands, saying, "Come along!" and off they went. However, you could not have called it walking! No, the children seemed to float along through the woods and meadows, while brightly feathered birds flew around them. Then the strange child took out a little golden horn, saying, "Now I'll play you a tune of farewell, but I'll come back tomorrow!" The child played, and the nightingales sang, but suddenly the notes of the horn and the birdsong died away, and all that could be heard was the rustling of the bushes into which the strange child had vanished.

"Tomorrow ... I'll be back tomorrow!" called a voice from very far away.

Felix and Christlieb had never felt so happy in all their lives! "Oh, if only it were tomorrow now!" they said, as they hurried home to tell their parents what had happened in the forest.

"I'd be inclined to think the children had been dreaming!" said Sir Thaddeus to his lady, when Felix and Christlieb had told their tale. "Yet how could they both have had the same dream at once? I don't know what to make of it at all!"

"Oh," said his wife, "I dare say this strange child is only Gottlieb the schoolmaster's son, from the next village, and he has been over here filling the children's heads with nonsense!"

But Sir Thaddeus did not think so. He asked Felix and Christlieb what the child looked like and what clothes it wore. They both agreed that the child had a face white as a lily, cheeks pink as roses, lips red as cherries, bright blue eyes and

golden curls, but as for its clothes, all they could say was that they were nothing like Gottlieb's striped blue jacket and trousers and black leather cap. And while Christlieb said the child had a lovely gauzy dress made of rose petals, Felix claimed that it wore a suit of light green, like young leaves in the sunshine. Moreover, said Felix, the boy was no schoolmaster's son: he knew far too much about hunting, and would be a great huntsman himself some day.

"Oh, Felix!" Christlieb interrupted. "How can you say that dear little girl will be a huntsman? She may know a good deal about hunting, but I'm sure she knows how to keep house even better, or she couldn't have dressed those dolls so prettily for me!"

So Felix thought the strange child was a boy, and Christlieb thought the strange child was a girl, and they could not agree.

"I need only follow the children into the forest to see what sort of child this really is," said Sir Thaddeus to his lady. "Yet I feel as if I might be spoiling some great pleasure for them, so I won't do it."

Next day the strange child was there again, waiting to show Felix and Christlieb the most wonderful things, talking to the trees, the bushes, the brook and the flowers, who all answered back in language the children could understand. They joined in the conversation happily themselves. At evening, when the nightingales began to sing, the strange child took them flying through the air, towards glowing sunset clouds like beautiful buildings. "My castles in the air!" said the child. "But we won't get there today!" Then, unexpectedly, Felix and Christlieb found themselves back home with their mother and their father, not quite sure how they had come there.

ABOUT THE STRANGE CHILD'S HOME One day Felix and Christlieb were sitting in a beautiful pavilion that the strange child had built out of tall lilies, glowing roses and bright tulips. "I say, old fellow, where do you really come from?" Felix asked. "And where is it you go when you vanish so fast that we can hardly tell how?"

"Oh, dear little girl," Christlieb put in, "did you know that Mother thinks you're Gottlieb, the schoolmaster's son?"

"Be quiet, you silly thing!" said Felix. "If Mother had ever seen this nice boy she'd never take him for Gottlieb! Now, do tell me where you live. Then we can come and visit you at home in winter, when it's too cold and stormy to walk in the woods."

"Yes, yes!" said Christlieb. "Tell us where you live, and who your parents are, and most important of all, tell us your name!"

The strange child looked grave, almost sad, and said, sighing, "Dear children, why ask where I live? I come to play with you daily – isn't that enough? I could say I live beyond those blue mountains that look like clouds in the distance, yet if you were to walk for days until at last you reached them, you would see another range just as far away, and another beyond that, and so on and on, and you would never reach my own country."

"Then you live hundreds of miles away, and you're only a visitor here?" said Christlieb sadly.

"Listen, dear Christlieb," said the strange child. "When you really want me, here I am directly, bringing you wonderful things from my home! Isn't that as good as if we were playing there together?"

"Not quite," said Felix. "Your home must be a marvellous place, and whatever you say I'm setting off to go there as soon as I can. I'll get to it somehow!"

"Why, so you will!" said the strange child, laughing merrily. "And if you're so determined, it's as good as if you were really there already! My own country is more beautiful than I can say, and my mother is the queen of it and rules over all its wonders."

"Then you're a prince!" "Then you're a princess!" cried Felix and Christlieb in amazement, both at once.

"Yes, indeed I am!" said the strange child.

"And I suppose you live in a wonderful palace?" Felix went on.

"Yes," said the child, "my mother's palace is even more beautiful than those shining castles you saw in the air. It rises high into the blue sky on slender columns of pure crystal, and the vault of heaven rests on them as its roof. Bright golden clouds sail below that roof, the sun rises and sets in the rosy light of dawn and dusk, and the sparkling stars dance their chiming round. Dear children, you must have heard of fairies, and by now you will have guessed that my mother is a fairy, the most powerful fairy of all. She loves everything that lives and grows on earth, and children most of all, so the parties she gives for children in her kingdom are the best you ever saw. Her courtier spirits fly boldly through the clouds to stretch a shimmering rainbow from one end of her palace to the other, and under it they set up my mother's throne, which is made of pure diamonds, although they look like lilies, pinks, and roses and smell just as sweet. Her musicians play their golden harps and crystal cymbals, and her singers strike up their song: they are beautiful birds, bigger than eagles, with purple feathers, and as soon as the music begins everything in the palace comes to life. Thousands of children dance and play and shout for joy, chasing each other and throwing flowers, climbing trees and letting the winds rock them back and forth, picking delicious golden fruits, and playing with the tame deer and other creatures that come bounding out of the thickets to meet them. They race boldly up and down the rainbow, or clamber up on beautiful golden pheasants to ride them through the clouds."

"Oh, how lovely! Do take us to your country, and we'll stay there forever!" cried Felix and Christlieb in delight.

"No," said the strange child, "I can't take you there. It is too far away, and you would need to fly as well as I do." And then the child went on to tell them more about the fairy country, and the queen's deadly enemy, a wicked spirit who became her minister and tried to hurt the children, the singing birds, and the tame beasts. At last he tried to seize her throne, appearing in the shape of a monstrous fly, and then everyone recognized him as the wicked Pepser, King of the Gnomes. "However," said the child, "the Pheasant Prince fought a battle with Pepser and drove him out, and soon all was well with my mother's kingdom again – but Pepser follows me when I leave it, hoping to harm me. And that, my dears, is why I often have to vanish all of a sudden. If I were to take you to my home, Pepser would be sure to see us and kill us."

Felix and Christlieb ran home to tell their parents this tale – but they stopped dead when they saw Sir Thaddeus of Brakel come out to meet them with a strange man at his side. "This is the tutor your kind uncle has sent," said Sir Thaddeus. "Greet him politely, like good children!" But the children could not move. They had never seen so strange a figure before! The man was not much taller than Felix himself, but he was squat, with thin little spidery legs, a misshapen head, and an ugly face: his nose was too long, he had fat, reddish cheeks and a wide mouth, and small, shiny, protuberant eyes. He wore a black wig and was dressed in black from head to foot, and his name was Master Inkspot.

"Good gracious, children, what's the matter with you?" said their mother. "Master Inkspot will think you very rude and ignorant! Come along, shake hands with him!"

So the children did as they were asked, but when the tutor shook hands with them they shrank back, screaming. He laughed out loud, and showed them that he had a needle hidden in his palm, to prick them with.

"But why, my dear Master Inkspot?" asked Sir Thaddeus, a little angrily.

"Oh, it's just my way, and I can't seem to give it up!" said the tutor, and he put his hands on his hips and laughed and laughed. It was a most unpleasant sound, like a cracked rattle.

"Well, you have quite a sense of humor, Master Inkspot," said Sir Thaddeus, but neither he nor his family felt very happy about it.

"And are you two clever children?" asked the tutor. "Let's see!" So saying, he began to ask Felix and Christlieb the kind of questions their cousins could answer, and when it turned out that they didn't know the answers themselves he cried angrily, "Here's a fine thing! What – you know nothing? I can see there's work to be done here!"

Both Felix and Christlieb could write neatly, and they read a great deal, and could tell good stories out of the old books Sir Thaddeus had given them, but Master Inkspot said all that was nonsense. So now there was no more playing in the forest! The children had to sit indoors nearly all day long, learning their lessons. They felt as if they heard the strange child calling to them. "Come out, oh, come out and play! Don't you want to play with me any more?" Then they paid no more attention to their tutor, and at last they could not help jumping up to run out into the woods. The tutor ran after them, and there was a scuffle in the doorway, with Sultan the dog joining in on the children's side. Sir Thaddeus came along to separate them all, and said that the tutor was to go out in the woods with the children once a day.

Master Inkspot did not think much of that. "If you had a garden, well and good!" said he. "But what in the world are we to do in the wild woods?"

"Yes," said the children, "what in the world is Master Inkspot to do in our own dear forest?"

Out they all three went, however, and Felix asked the tutor, "Don't you like our woods, Sir, and the birds and the flowers?"

Master Inkspot made a face. "A stupid sort of place!" he said. "There's no proper path, you only tear your stockings, and there's nothing to be said for the screeching of those stupid birds! I don't mind flowers so long as they're in pots indoors, but these useless wild flowers don't even smell sweet!" And so saying, he bent down, pulled up a whole clump of lilies of the valley, roots and all, and threw it away into the bushes.

The children felt as if a cry of pain went through the forest, and Christlieb could

not help shedding tears, while Felix ground his teeth. Then a little greenfinch flew right past the tutor's nose, settled on a branch, and sang a merry song.

"I do believe that's a mocking bird!" said the tutor. He picked up a stone, threw it at the greenfinch, and hit the poor bird so hard that it fell down dead.

This was too much for Felix. "What did that poor bird ever do to hurt you, Master Inkspot?" he cried angrily. "Now you've killed it! Oh, dear strange child, please come and let us fly away with you!"

Sobbing, Christlieb joined in too. "Please, dear child, come and save us, or Master Inkspot will kill us like the flowers and the birds!"

"Child? What's all this about a child?" said the tutor.

Then there was a rustling in the bushes, and the children heard the sound of sad, heartrending notes, like the faint chime of bells echoing far away. A bright, shining cloud floated low, and in it they saw the strange child's lovely face. But the child was wringing its hands, and tears like bright pearls were running down its rosy cheeks. "Oh, dear playmates," wailed the strange child, "I can't come to you any more, and you will never see me again! Goodbye, goodbye! You poor children – Pepser the gnome has you in his power! Goodbye, goodbye!"

And the strange child floated up into the air again.

But the children heard the most fearsome humming and hawing and buzzing and snarling behind them. Master Inkspot had turned himself into a horrible, huge fly, and it was a dreadful sight to see him, for he still had a human face, and had even kept some of his clothes on. He rose slowly into the air, flying with difficulty. He was obviously trying to follow the strange child. Felix and Christlieb ran out of the forest in horror and dismay, and they dared not look up until they were in the open fields. Then they saw a shining spot among the clouds, twinkling like a star. It was coming lower, it grew larger and larger, and they heard a noise like the sound of trumpets blowing. Soon they could see that the star was a beautiful and magnificent bird with glittering golden plumage. It was coming down over the forest, flapping its mighty wings and singing aloud.

"Look!" cried Felix. "It's the Pheasant Prince, and he will peck Master Inkspot to death. The strange child is safe, and so are we! Come along, Christlieb, let's go home and tell Father."

Sir Thaddeus and his lady were sitting outside the door of their little house, with their supper on a table before them. It was a good bowl of delicious milk, and a plate of bread and butter.

"Where can Master Inkspot be with the children, all this time?" said Sir Thaddeus. "First he shuts himself indoors and won't go into the woods, now he won't come out of them! He's a very strange man, is this Master Inkspot, and I'm beginning to think it would be better if he had never come here at all."

"Dear husband," said his wife, "I feel just the same! I was glad that your cousin wanted to do something for the good of our children, but I don't care for Master Inkspot. Learned he may be, but he's very greedy too! He has only to see a glass with a few dregs of milk or beer, and he drains it! If the box of sugar is left open he's at it directly, nibbling away until I slam the lid down before his very nose! And then off he goes, so angrily, buzzing and humming and hawing in the strangest way!"

Just then Felix and Christlieb came running home through the birch trees. Felix kept shouting, "Hooray, hooray! The Pheasant Prince has pecked Master Inkspot to death!"

"Oh, Mother!" cried Christlieb breathlessly. "Oh, Master Inkspot isn't Master Inkspot at all. He's Pepser, the King of the Gnomes, and he's really a horrible huge fly wearing a wig and shoes and stockings!"

The parents stared at their children as they went on to tell the whole story of the strange child's mother, who was the fairy queen, and Pepser the King of the Gnomes, and the Pheasant Prince.

"Whoever put such nonsense into your heads? Or did you dream it all?" asked Sir Thaddeus. But then he grew very grave and thoughtful. "Felix," said he at last, "Felix, you're a sensible boy, and I may as well tell you I myself thought this tutor a strange fellow, from the very start. Your mother doesn't like him either, because he is so greedy, always nibbling sweet things, and humming and buzzing so nastily as he goes about it, so he won't be staying long with us. But my dear boy, just suppose there really could be such things as gnomes – even so , could a tutor be a fly?"

Felix looked Sir Thaddeus straight in the face, and said, "I'd never have thought so, Father, and I dare say I wouldn't have believed it if the strange child hadn't told me so – and if I hadn't seen it with my own eyes. But now I know that Pepser is a nasty fly, and was only pretending to be Master Inkspot the tutor! Why, Father, didn't I once hear Master Inkspot himself tell you he was a high flyer

when he was at school? And I don't suppose a person can change his nature! Then, just think how greedy he is, always after anything sweet, as Mother says! Isn't that exactly like a fly? And there's his nasty humming and buzzing too!"

"Hush!" said Sir Thaddeus of Brakel, quite angrily. "Whatever Master Inkspot may be, one thing is certain: no Pheasant Prince has pecked him to death, for here he comes out of the woods!"

At that the children screamed, and ran indoors for safety. Sure enough, Master Inkspot was coming up the avenue of birch trees, but looking very wild, with his eyes sparkling and his wig untidy, humming and buzzing horribly as he wove from side to side, leaping up in the air and knocking his head against the trees. He came up to the doorway of the house and fell upon the bowl of milk. It overflowed and he lapped the milk up with a disgusting slurping sound.

"Good gracious me, Master Inkspot!" cried Sir Thaddeus of Brakel's lady. "Whatever are you doing?"

"Are you mad, sir?" asked Sir Thaddeus. "Is the Devil after you, or what?"

Taking no notice at all, the tutor got out of the bowl of milk and settled on the bread and butter, shaking out his coat tails and smoothing them into shape with his thin little legs. Then, humming louder than ever, he flung himself against the door, but he couldn't get into the house. He swayed back and forth as if he were drunk, battering himself against the windows so that they whirred and rang.

"Now, now, sir!" cried Sir Thaddeus. "This is no way to behave! You'll be sorry for this – just you wait!" He tried to catch the tutor by the tails of his coat, but Master Inkspot got away, and then Felix came running out of the house with the big fly swatter and gave it to his father. "Here, Father!" he cried. "Take this and kill that ugly Pepser!"

And Sir Thaddeus really did take the fly swatter, and went for the tutor with it! Felix and Christlieb and their mother were waving table napkins about, driving the tutor back and forth, while Sir Thaddeus rained down blows, although unfortunately they all missed, since Master Inkspot, buzzing wildly, never kept still for a moment.

At last, however, Sir Thaddeus managed to grab the tutor by his coat tails. Master Inkspot fell to the ground, groaning, but just as Sir Thaddeus was about to swat him for the second time, he rose up again, stronger than ever, made for the birch trees, humming and buzzing, and no more was seen of him.

"We're well rid of that disagreeable Master Inkspot!" said Sir Thaddeus. "He'll never darken my doors again!"

"No, indeed he won't!" agreed his lady. "A tutor, of all people, with such shocking manners! Boasting of his learning and jumping into a bowl of milk … a fine sort of tutor, I must say!"

And Felix and Christlieb shouted for joy. "Hooray! Father hit Master Inkspot with the fly swatter, and now he's gone for good – hooray, hooray!"

WHAT SIR THADDEUS AND HIS LADY SAID ABOUT THE STRANGE CHILD So all seemed well, and yet, much as the children hoped to see the strange child again, they never did. And when they went into the woods, the forest seemed to be haunted by the broken toys they had thrown away, for those toys were all creatures and servants of Pepser the gnome (or Master Inkspot the tutor), who still went buzzing about the forest. So Felix and Christlieb gave up walking in the forest, and their father, Sir Thaddeus, was not well.

"I don't know what the matter is," he said to his lady one day, "but I could almost believe that wicked Master Inkspot is the cause of it. Ever since I hit him with the fly swatter and drove him off, my limbs have felt as if they were made of lead."

Indeed, Sir Thaddeus of Brakel was growing paler and wearier every day. He no longer strode over his land as he used to do, but would sit for hours, lost in thought, and then he asked Felix and Christlieb to tell him about the strange child. They talked eagerly, and he would smile in a melancholy manner, while tears came into his eyes.

Felix and Christlieb were unhappy because they did not see the strange child any more, and they were afraid to go into the forest because of the sinister toys haunting it. Their father noticed that. "Come, let's go into the woods together, and Master Inkspot's evil creatures will do you no harm!" he told them one fine morning. He took his children by the hand and they went out into the woods. The forest was lovelier than ever, full of sweet scents, birdsong and sunshine. They sat down in the grass, among the fragrant flowers.

"Dear children," said Sir Thaddeus, "I must tell you now, for it cannot be put off any longer, that I myself once knew that strange and lovely child who showed you such marvels here in the forest. When I was your age, the child visited me too, and we played wonderful games together. I don't remember now how it was that the child left me, nor how I came to forget it so completely that when you told me your tale I didn't believe it. Yet somehow I often sensed vaguely that you were telling the truth. But now I have been remembering the happy days of my youth, and that lovely and magical child, and the same longing you feel yourselves filled my breast, but it will break my heart! I feel that this is the last time I shall ever sit under these trees. Children dear, I must soon leave you. And when I am dead, keep the strange child in your minds!"

Felix and Christlieb were grief-stricken. They wept, and cried, "Oh no, Father, you won't die! You will stay with us for a long, long time, and play with the strange child too!"

However, the very next day Sir Thaddeus lay sick in bed, and a tall, thin man came to feel his pulse, and said all would be well. All was not well, for on the third day after that, Sir Thaddeus was dead, and his wife and children mourned him.

Before long, when he had been buried, a couple of ugly men who looked almost the same as Master Inkspot came to the house, and told Sir Thaddeus's lady that they were taking possession of the property. Count Cyprian had lent his late cousin more than the place was worth, and now the Count wanted his money back. So the poor lady, in dire poverty, had to leave the pretty village of Brakelheim. She decided to go to a relative of hers who lived not far away, and she and Felix and Christlieb made little bundles of what few clothes they were allowed to keep and left their home, shedding many tears.

After walking for some time through the woods, they could hear the wild rushing of the forest river which they would soon have to cross. All at once, the children's poor mother, weighed down by her bitter grief, fell fainting to the ground. Felix and Christlieb went down on their knees, wailing, "Oh, poor unhappy children that we are, will no one take pity on us?"

And then the distant rushing of the river seemed to become sweet music, the bushes moved with a mysterious rustling sound, and soon the whole forest was bathed in a wonderful, sparkling light. The strange child stepped out of the sweetly scented leaves, surrounded by such dazzling brightness that the children had to shut their eyes. Then they felt a soft touch, and heard the strange child's voice saying, "Don't grieve, dear playmates! Do you think I don't love you any more, or that I could leave you? You may not see me with your outward eyes, but I'll always be with you, and do all I can to make you glad and happy. Keep me in your hearts as you have done until now, and neither the wicked Pepser nor any other enemy can harm you! Only love me always and love me truly!"

"We will, oh, we will!" cried Felix and Christlieb. "We love you with all our hearts!"

When they could open their eyes again, the strange child had gone, but so had all their grief, and they felt heavenly joy deep within them. Slowly, their mother sat up. "Oh, dear children!" she said. "I dreamed of you! I seemed to see you standing in a sparkling golden light, and it comforted me most wonderfully!"

There was joy in the children's eyes, and their cheeks were glowing. They told their mother how the strange child had been there to console them, and she said, "I don't know why, but I believe your tale today, and nor do I know why it takes my pain and grief away, but so it is! Let us pluck up our courage and go on."

Her relative welcomed them in kindly, and it was all as the strange child had promised. Everything Felix and Christlieb did turned out so well that they, and their mother, were very happy.

And for a long time to come, they played with the strange child in sweet dreams, and the strange child never failed to bring them marvels and wonders from its own country.

E. T. A. Hoffmann lived from 1776 to 1822. His initials stand for Ernst Theodor Amadeus, and the name itself tells us something of the writer's character, for the the third name was his own choice as an homage to Wolfgang Amadeus Mozart, replacing his original third Christian name of Wilhelm.

Although he was only forty-six when he died, he crammed an amazing quantity of work into his short life. He began his career by studying law, but soon took to art, music and literature instead. In fact he was over thirty when he first began to write for publication, and by the time of his death he had written, as well as music criticism, two novels (one unfinished when he died) and about fifty stories, most of them quite long.

THE STRANGE CHILD was written and first published in 1817. Hoffmann republished it in 1819, in the second volume of his four-volume collection of stories. It is less well known than his familiar tale, THE NUTCRACKER, but like that story it is full of magic, mystery and fantasy. Both stories may have been written with the children of Hoffmann's friend Julius Eduard Hitzig, a bookseller and publisher, in mind. After Hoffmann's death, Hitzig published a biography of him.

This text is considerably shortened from Hoffmann's original story, but aims to retain the spirit of his fantasy as reflected in the pictures by Lisbeth Zwerger.